JURASSIC PECK

Read more Kung Pow Chicken books!

1 KUNG POW CHICKEN★ LET'S GET CRACKING! Cyndi Marko SCHOLASTIC

2 KUNG POW CHICKEN★ BOK! BOK! BOOM! Cyndi Marko SCHOLASTIC

3 KUNG POW CHICKEN★ THE BIRDY SNATCHERS Cyndi Marko SCHOLASTIC

4 KUNG POW CHICKEN★ HEROES ON THE SIDE Cyndi Marko SCHOLASTIC

5 KUNG POW CHICKEN★ JURASSIC PECK Cyndi Marko SCHOLASTIC

KUNG POW CHICKEN★

JURASSIC PECK

Cyndi Marko

BRANCHES

SCHOLASTIC INC.

For Hannah
Girl Power!

Library of Congress Cataloging-in-Publication Data
Marko, Cyndi, author, illustrator.
Jurassic peck / Cyndi Marko.
Description: First edition. | New York : Branches/Scholastic, 2020. |
Series: Kung Pow Chicken ; 5 | Summary: An accident in Professor Quack's lab sends Gordon Blue (otherwise known as Kung Pow Chicken) and his companions, Egg Drop and Beak Girl, back to dinosaur times, where they meet Dr. Strangebok, an evil chicken who wants to bring dinosaurs to Fowladelphia and take over the city—and the three superheroes, with help from a friendly dinosaur named Sweet Tooth, must find a way to stop her before she turns the city into a buffet lunch for her dinos.
Identifiers: LCCN 2019041180 | ISBN 9781338596649 (paperback) |
ISBN 9781338596656 (library binding) | ISBN 9781338596663 (ebk)
Subjects: LCSH: Chickens—Juvenile fiction. | Dinosaurs—Juvenile fiction.
| Superheroes—Juvenile fiction. | Time travel—Juvenile fiction. |
Humorous stories. | CYAC: Chickens—Fiction. | Dinosaurs—Fiction. |
Superheroes—Fiction. | Time travel—Fiction. | Humorous stories. |
LCGFT: Superhero fiction. | Humorous fiction.
Classification: LCC PZ7.M33968 Ju 2020 | DDC 813.6 [Fic]—dc23
LC record available at https://lccn.loc.gov/2019041180

10 9 8 7 6 5 4 3 2 1   20 21 22 23 24

Printed in China   62

First edition, September 2020

Edited by Katie Carella
Book design by Marissa Asuncion

TABLE OF CONTENTS

1 The Birds Are Back in Town ..1

2 Chicken-saurus Rex 11

3 Time and Space Go Phlooey .. 19

4 What Time Is It? 29

5 Dino-mite! 39

6 Escape Time! 47

7 Back to the Future 55

8 Birdzilla!!! 61

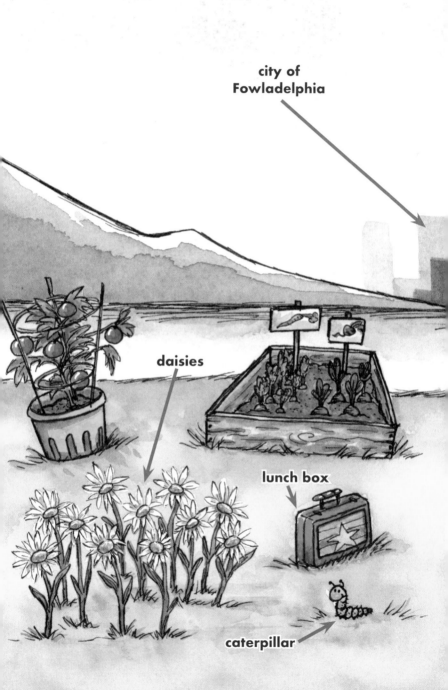

city of
Fowladelphia

daisies

lunch box

caterpillar

wattle

school tie

tail feathers

seeds

Gordon Blue seemed like an ordinary chicken.

He lived in the ordinary city of Fowladelphia . . .

With his <u>mostly</u> ordinary family.

But Gordon had a <u>super</u> secret that no one else knew . . .

SNEAK SNEAK

Well, his younger brother, Benny, and their Uncle Quack knew Gordon's secret. But no one else did.

His leotard is <u>so</u> tight.

But being <u>super</u> wasn't easy.

Fighting bad guys made you late for dinner.

Super suits rubbed in all the wrong places,
which led to embarrassing talks.

And it was hard to keep the <u>super</u> secret from your friends.

Annie Beakly was Gordon Blue's best friend.

But . . .

I have a secret, too! I'm the superhero known as Beak Girl!

Beak Girl was a pain in Kung Pow Chicken's tail feathers.

I can out-super Kung Pow Chicken any day!

Gordon just got back from doing superhero stuff in New Yolk City.

Now Kung Pow Chicken was ready to get back to protecting his <u>own</u> city from bad guys.

With help from his trusty sidekick!

But first, Gordon had to go back to ordinary old school.

Gordon's teacher, Mr. Giblets, was more cheerful than usual.

Gordon longed for excitement. But what could happen on an ordinary old school field trip?

Chicken-saurus Rex 2

Gordon grew even more bored on the school bus. But Benny was having fun playing with his toys.

Gordon slumped down in his seat. He wished he had a bad guy to fight.

Mr. Giblets led the students off the bus and into the Museum of Chicken History.

This way to the dinosaur hall!

DINOSAUR HALL

That's an archaeopteryx. They are only a bit bigger than chickens! Scientists think they were the first bird!

JURASSIC DINOSAURS

Stegosaurus

Allosaurus

Brachiosaurus

Archaeopteryx
(aar·kee·aa p·√r·uhks)

This is so cool!!

Best day ever!

Worst day ever.

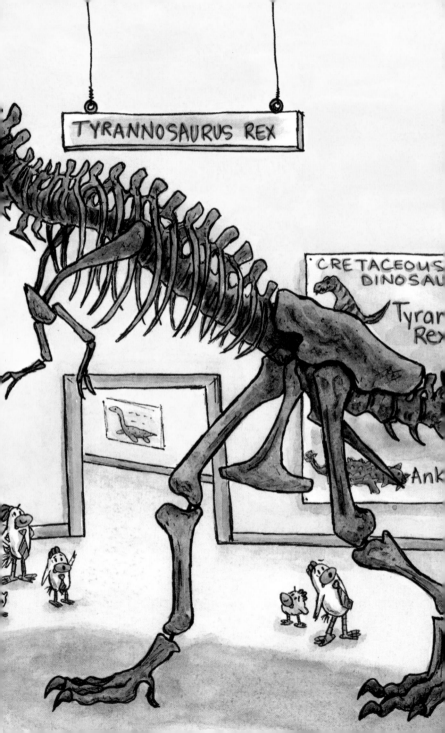

Mr. Giblets told the class the <u>best</u> fun fact about dinosaurs.

Then a chicken with a strange hammer on her belt entered the dinosaur hall.

Hello, students. I'm Dr. Strangebok.

I am a paleontologist—that's a dinosaur scientist.

Did you know that many dinosaurs had feathers? They were like big birds.

Somehow, Gordon made it through the rest of the field trip. He was happy when they finally got on the bus to go home.

On Saturday morning, Gordon and Benny rode their Big Wheel to Uncle Quack's lab.

Yahoo! We get to hang out all day with Uncle Quack! That's never boring!

Right? There's always a chance something in the lab could explode!

19

Uncle Quack let Gordon and Benny watch their favorite cartoon and eat cereal while he did some work in the lab.

Rocket Rooster will save you!

But then Uncle Quack turned the TV off.

Boys, change into your super suits! I want to get to know Beak Girl better, so I've asked her over for tea and science stuff.

Yay! Beak Girl!

BOOP!

GROAN...

Gordon and Benny slipped into their super
suits. One of them wasn't happy about it.

DING-DONG!

Uncle Quack led Beak Girl
into the lab and served
everyone tea and cookies.

Isn't this nice? I love tea!

Next, it's time for
science stuff.

Uncle Quack pulled a gadget from behind his back.

This is my newest gadget! The Any-Time-Machine™. Enter a date, and it shows a hologram of the <u>neato</u> stuff that happened that day.

Wow! That's when Neil Wingstrong walked on the moon!

BEEP!

Oops. It needs a new battery . . .

Plutonium   Batteries

That's not a battery!

But it was too late. Professor Quack put plutonium in the Any-Time-Machine™. Then everything got weird.

RRRII

Uh-oh! I just ripped a hole in time and space! That's a giant wormhole!

The three superheroes rocketed through time and space. The history of <u>chickenkind</u> flashed before their eyes.

AHHHHHH!

WHUMP!

Meanwhile, back at the lab...

Weird. That's never happened before.

The dizzy superheroes peeked out of the giant fern.

Where are we?

More like <u>when</u> are we?

We're not in Fowladelphia anymore.

Just then, a giant spider dangled in front of Kung Pow Chicken.

Kung Pow Chicken freaked out. A little.

BWAWK!

BWAWK!

Kung Pow Chicken, Beak Girl, and Egg Drop heard a strange bokking noise. They ducked down just before a pair of small birdlike dinosaurs passed by them.

The heroes knew there was something not quite right about these dinosaurs.

Suddenly, Kung Pow Chicken's Beak-Phone™ buzzed. It was Professor Quack.

Kung Pow Chicken, Egg Drop, and Beak Girl went back to following the two collared dinosaurs.

The heroes pushed through some ferns and reached the edge of a clearing. Many dinosaurs stood there—and they were <u>all</u> wearing blinking collars!

Just then, a huge shadow blocked out the sun.

AHHH! T. Rex!

TINGLE!

Kung Pow Chicken prepared to be dino-dinner.

Dino-mite!

5

A small birdlike creature stepped into sight.

Hi! My name is Sweet-Tooth!

You're not a T. Rex!

T. Rexes won't be around for another 70 to 80 million years.

She's an archaeopteryx.

Archaeopteryx
(aar-kee-oo-p-ter-uhks)

Now Kung Pow Chicken was cranky.

I will defeat Dr. Strangebok and rescue the collared dinos without your help.

Not if we beat you to it. And don't expect us to save _your_ butt.

Come on, Egg Drop . . . We have a bad guy to battle.

Come on, Sweet-Tooth . . .

Kung Pow Chicken rushed into the clearing.
Egg Drop followed Kung Pow Chicken into battle.

Kung Pow Chicken and Egg Drop fought bravely.

The dinosaurs' collars began to blink faster.

BWAWK! BWAWK! BWAWK!

Then the dinosaurs attacked. Kung Pow Chicken and Egg Drop tried to escape.

AHHHHH! Run!

Ham and dino eggs!

STOMP! STOMP!

But there was nowhere to run. So they turned to fight.

But they got their butts kicked.

Those must be Sweet-Tooth's sisters!

You're a good egg, Egg Drop. You're the best sidekick a hero could have. And the best brother. I hope we get out of this.

BLUSH!

Escape Time!

Dr. Strangebok ordered the dinosaurs to get ready for something big. Meanwhile, Kung Pow Chicken and Egg Drop struggled to get free.

Keep wiggling, Egg Drop. The rope is getting looser.

Dr. Strangebok glared at the trapped heroes.

Well, well, well.
The great Kung Pow Chicken.
And his little egg, too.

You're a bad bird,
Dr. Strangebok.

Why are you dino-napping
all those dinosaurs?

Dr. Strangebok took a deep breath. Then she told the heroes her naughty plans.

I'm sending these dinosaurs back to the future, where they will help me take over Fowladelphia. And then the world!

Dr. Strangebok took out a weird gadget and started zapping it in all directions. Mini wormholes opened up all over the clearing.

Beak Girl and Sweet-Tooth crawled out from behind a nearby fern. Then Sweet-Tooth chewed through the ropes holding Kung Pow Chicken and Egg Drop.

Hurry! Dr. Strangebok is getting away with the dinos!

Kung Pow Chicken was free! But it was too late. Dr. Strangebok and the dinosaurs were gone. And the heroes were still stuck in the past.

My sisters!

Just then, a wormhole RIPPED open next to Kung Pow Chicken. Professor Quack's voice called out of it.

> Quick! I can't hold this hole open forever!

> Professor Quack?! You fixed the Any-Time-Machine™!

> Let's go!

> I'm coming, too!

The heroes jumped into the wormhole. They had to save the chickens of Fowladelphia.

Kung Pow Chicken and his friends popped out of
the wormhole onto the roof of Quack Labs.

Dinosaurs roamed the streets. More collared creatures filled the sky. One even swam in the river. The chickens of Fowladelphia ran through the streets <u>bokking</u> in fear.

While Professor Quack gathered his best gadgets, Kung Pow Chicken and Beak Girl filled him in on what had happened in the past. Professor Quack bokked when he heard Dr. Strangebok's naughty plans.

Then Professor Quack turned to Kung Pow Chicken.

Kung Pow Chicken grew
to dino size!

I'm big enough to stop the dinos now. But I don't want to hurt them. How do I rescue them from Dr. Strangebok?

You need to defeat Dr. Strangebok first. Use my Bok-Stop-5000™. It will turn her strange boks into kazoo noises. Then she will no longer be able to control the dinos.

And remember, your great-great-and-so-on grandparents were T. Rexes! You can do this.

STOMP! STOMP! STOP!

Ack! Dino-size wedgie!

Kung Pow Chicken stomped (carefully!) through the streets of Fowladelphia.

Where is Dr. Strangebok?

At last, Kung Pow Chicken spotted her. She was riding a collared dinosaur. And that dinosaur was about to <u>eat</u> an innocent chicken!

I'll save you!

BWAWK!

BOK

Kung Pow Chicken and the other heroes were all in place. Now it was time to battle!

Kung Pow Chicken flung his
giant-size Beak-A-Rang™ at
Dr. Strangebok's dinosaur.

The Beak-A-Rang™ wrapped around the
dinosaur's powerful legs.

Then Kung Pow Chicken picked up
Dr. Strangebok in his giant fist. He slipped the
Bok-Stop-5000™ on the naughty chicken.

Dr. Strangebok tried to bok out orders to the
collared dinosaurs, but all that came out of her
beak was—

Without her strange bok, Dr. Strangebok couldn't control the dinosaurs anymore.

Next, Kung Pow Chicken stomped on Dr. Strangebok's time-travel gadget so it could never be used for bad-guy stuff again.

SMASH!

Finally, he lifted the roof off the city jail and dropped Dr. Strangebok into an empty cell.

The heroes worked together to remove all of Dr. Strangebok's crummy collars.

Now let's go find Professor Quack!

Professor Quack set the Any-Time-Machine™ to DINO-TIMES. It was time to send everyone home. But Egg Drop was sad. He didn't want to say good-bye.

Sweet-Tooth is a great teammate. Can she stay?

I'm sorry, Egg Drop. Everyone has to go back to their own time.

Egg Drop, I like you, too. But my sisters and I have to get home. If we're late for dinner, our mom will ground us.

We know what that's like!

Come visit anytime!

Professor Quack pushed the button on the Any-Time-Machine™.

Next, Professor Quack set the Big-Bird™ to Chicken-Little™. He zapped Kung Pow Chicken to turn him back to normal.

When Gordon and Benny got home, Mrs. Blue was waiting with cold dinner and a frown.

third grade photo

Cyndi Marko lives in Canada with her family.

When Cyndi was younger, she loved dinosaurs. She thought there might be dino bones buried in her backyard. She took a little shovel and started to dig. But all she found were big fat worms, and potatoes, and carrots and—oh no . . . Mom's poor garden! Then Cyndi had a lot of time to think about dinosaurs after being sent to her room.

Kung Pow Chicken is Cyndi's first children's book series.

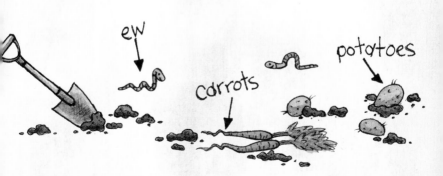

ew

carrots

potatoes

KUNG POW CHICKEN ★

Prove your superhero know-how!

Bok is an example of <u>onomatopoeia</u>, which means that it sounds like the thing it describes (like <u>meow</u>). What other words are like this?

When do Kung Pow Chicken's birdy senses first tell him that Dr. Strangebok is bad news?

On page 23, the Any-Time-Machine™ shows a hologram of Neil Wingstrong, who is based on a real person. What is this person's real name? Why is he famous?

Kung Pow Chicken wants to stop the dinosaurs from eating any chickens, but he does not want to hurt the dinosaurs. Why not?

Kung Pow Chicken, Egg Drop, and Beak Girl see amazing things in dino-times. Write about the things <u>you'd</u> see if you were there, too!